Marco Flamingo

Written and Illustrated by
Sheila Jarkins

Raven Tree Press
A Division of Delta Systems Co., Inc.
www.raventreepress.com

To my granddaughters, Anna and Taylor, with love — S.J.

Jarkins, Sheila.

    Marco Flamingo / written and illustrated by Sheila Jarkins; translated by
    Eida de la Vega = Marco Flamenco / escrito y ilustrado por Sheila Jarkins;
    traduccíon al español de Eida de la Vega. – 1 ed. – McHenry, IL ; Raven
    Tree Press, 2008.

        p. : cm.

English Edition
ISBN 978-1932748-53-6 hardcover
ISBN 978-1932748-57-4 paperback

Bilingual Edition
ISBN 978-09794462-5-2 hardcover
ISBN 978-09794462-6-9 paperback

Spanish Edition
ISBN 978-09794462-7-6 hardcover
ISBN 978-09794462-8-3 paperback

    SUMMARY: Marco is just a regular flamingo with one
    problem, he wants to be a winter bird. Watch what
    happens when he travels north for the winter.

        Audience: pre–K to 3rd grade.
        Bilingual full text English and Spanish, English–only and Spanish–only formats.

    1. Birds—Juvenile fiction. 2. Bilingual books.
    3. Picture books for children. 4. [Spanish
    language materials—Bilingual. I. Illus. Jarkins,
    Sheila , II. Title

            Library of Congress Control Number 2008920928

                    Printed in Taiwan
                 10 9 8 7 6 5 4 3 2 1
                      first edition

Marco waited under his favorite palm tree.
"Where are they?" he wondered.

"They're back! They're back!" Marco shouted.
"The snowbirds are back."

"There goes the peace and quiet."

"How many this year?"

4

Every year Marco had been curious about the snowbirds. So today he asked Goose, "Why do you come here every winter?" "Ah, it's paradise here, Flamingo. Never cold and NO SNOW." "What's snow?" Marco asked. "You don't want to know!" Goose replied.

But Marco did want to know about snow.
So, he asked a group of ducks,
"What's snow?"
"You don't want to know!" they replied.

Marco spent the night reading.
"I'll find out for myself," he thought.

The next morning Marco headed north.

13

He flew and he flew and he flew.

It got colder...

14

and colder...

and colder.

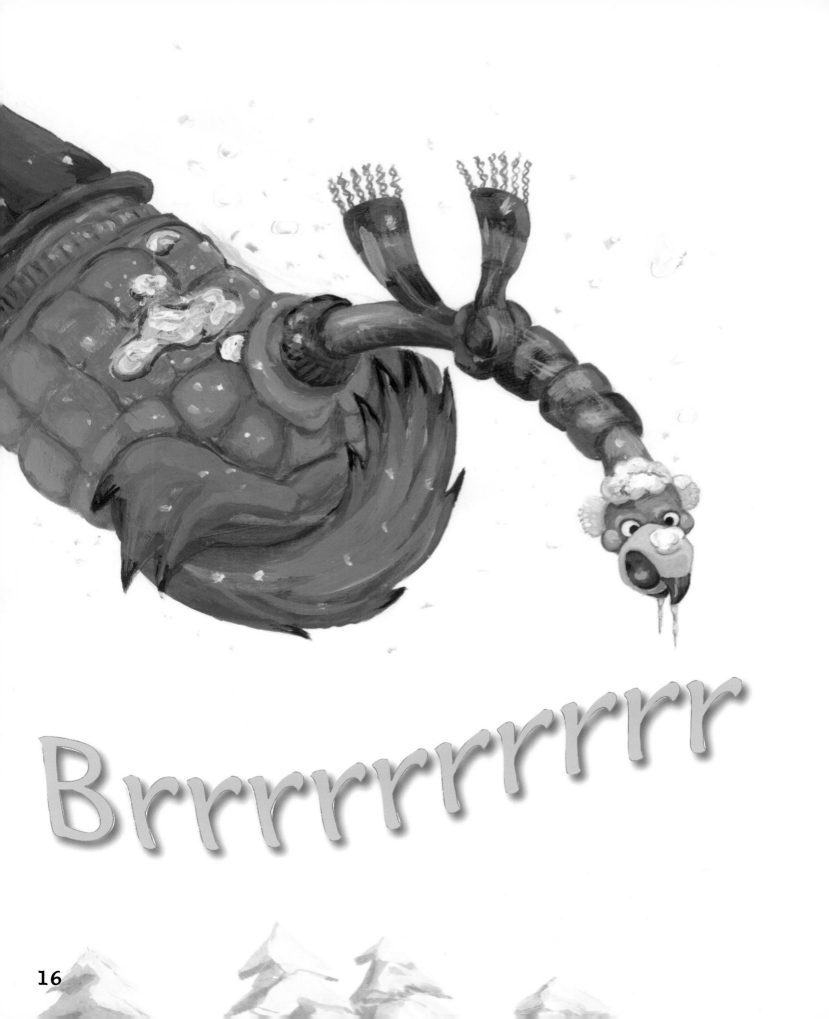

Brrrrrrrrrrr

He flew until he could fly no longer.

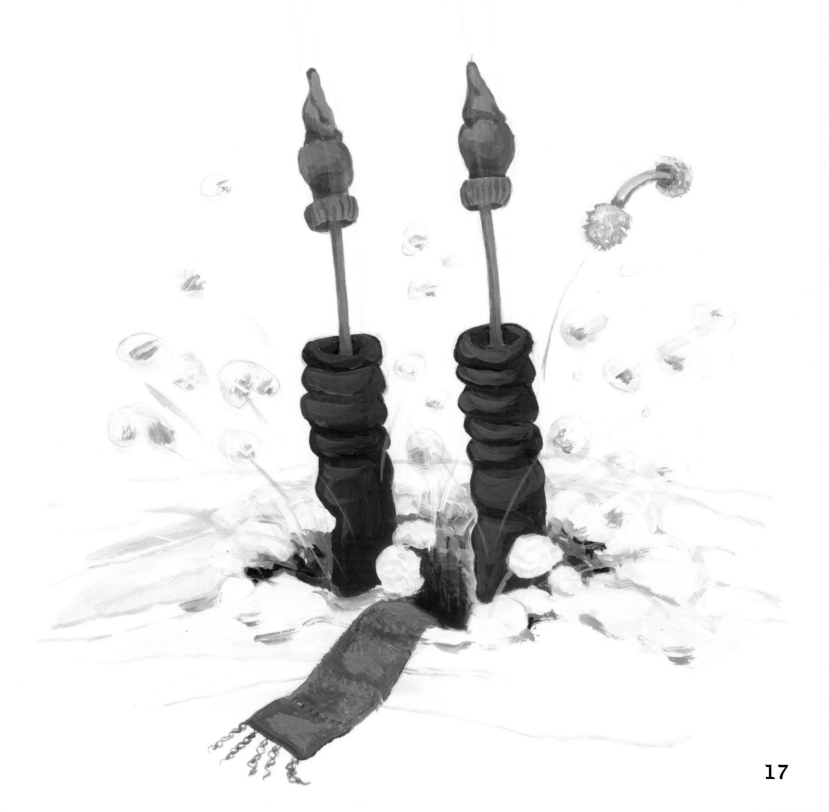

Wow!

"I love the snow!"

January 12

Dear Coral, Shelly and Webb:

I made it to a winter wonderland! Snow is everywhere. It sure is cold here, but I don't care. There are so many new things to do. I'm getting really good at them.

Sincerely, Marco

P.S. Please don't worry about me. I've got plenty to eat. I'll send another postcard soon.

P.P.S. Did Goose get a sunburn yet?

"Marco is certainly a rare bird."

Well, maybe not so rare after all.